Healthy Food for Dylan

By Sarah, Duchess of York   Illustrated by Ian Cunliffe

STERLING CHILDREN'S BOOKS
New York

STERLING CHILDREN'S BOOKS
New York

An Imprint of Sterling Publishing
387 Park Avenue South
New York, NY 10016

Library of Congress Cataloging-in-Publication Data Available

Lot#:
2 4 6 8 10 9 7 5 3 1
03/11
Published by Sterling Publishing Co., Inc.
387 Park Avenue South, New York, NY 10016
www.sterlingpublishing.com/kids
Story and illustrations © 2007 by Startworks Ltd.
"Ten Helpful Hints" © 2009 by Startworks Ltd.
Distributed in Canada by Sterling Publishing
c/o Canadian Manda Group, 165 Dufferin Street
Toronto, Ontario, Canada M6K 3H6
Distributed in Australia by Capricorn Link (Australia) Pty. Ltd.
P.O. Box 704, Windsor, NSW 2756, Australia

Sterling ISBN 978-1-4027-7400-3

For information about custom editions, special sales, premium and
corporate purchases, please contact Sterling Special Sales
Department at 800-805-5489 or specialsales@sterlingpublishing.com.

All children face many new experiences as they grow up, and helping them to understand and deal with each is one of the most demanding and rewarding things we do as parents. Helping Hand Books are for both children and parents to read, perhaps together. Each simple story describes a childhood experience and shows some of the ways in which to make it a positive one. I do hope these books encourage children and parents to talk about these sometimes difficult issues. Talking together goes a long way to finding a solution.

Sarah,

Sarah, Duchess of York

Dylan did not like mealtimes.
Mommy was always asking him to
try new foods. Dylan didn't like
to eat many kinds of food, which
made Mommy upset.

And that made Dylan upset, too.

Dylan's favorite food was French fries. If he could have them every day, he'd be the happiest boy in the world.

Mommy let him have French fries once in awhile. She said he also had to eat other things, like chicken and vegetables. Dylan was not happy about this. He wanted to eat French fries all day long!

One day, Dylan's cousin Abby and her parents came for lunch. Abby was going to stay with their family while her parents went on a short trip.

Dylan's mommy made a healthy lunch.

"Please don't make a fuss at lunchtime," Mommy told Dylan before everyone arrived. "Just eat your food like everyone else."

"Are we having French fries?" asked Dylan.

Mommy just frowned.

When Abby's family arrived, everyone sat down for lunch.
"Just a small portion for Abby, please," said Aunt Claire.
"She's been snacking on carrots in the car."
Everyone began to eat except for Dylan.

There were three sprigs of green broccoli in the middle of his plate. Dylan thought the broccoli looked like little bushes. They probably tasted like bushes, too!

"Eat your broccoli now," said Mommy firmly.

"No," said Dylan. "I'm full."

"Then you don't have any room for pie either," said Mommy.

"That's not fair!" said Dylan. He sulked for the rest of the meal.

After lunch, Aunt Claire told Dylan's mommy what Abby liked to eat.

"For breakfast, she has cereal, a piece of fruit, and a glass of milk. I always leave some sliced carrots in the fridge. Abby loves snacking on raw vegetables or a piece of fruit during the day."

"What about French fries?" Dylan's mommy asked nervously.

"I don't mind if she eats them once in a while," said Aunt Claire. "But I'd rather give Abby a few low-fat chips with a meal. They are just as tasty and she loves them. We often talk about which foods are good for her and why."

The next day, Dylan's mommy was preparing lunch. Abby asked if she could help.

"Cooking is boring," said Dylan.

"No, it isn't," said Abby. "Come and help us and you'll see how fun it can be."

Abby helped Dylan's mommy get some cheese slices, small tomatoes, and carrots out of the fridge.

"Now watch," said Abby. She put the cheese slices onto some bread and carefully cut the whole thing into a big circle with Dylan's mommy's help. Then she placed two small tomato halves on top for the eyes and a bigger one for the nose.

It looked like a face!

"What's his name?" asked Dylan with excitement. "I know! We'll call him Mr. Cheesy."

Dylan's mommy peeled and cut a carrot into very thin pieces. Abby arranged a mop of orange "hair" on Mr. Cheesy's head. A piece of celery was the finishing touch— a beaming smile.

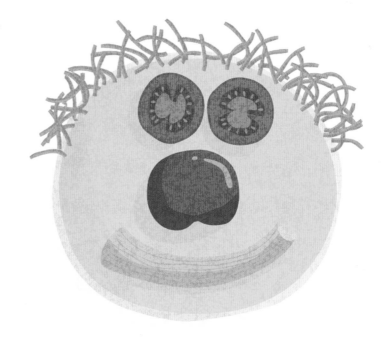

"Doesn't Mr. Cheesy look great?" asked Abby. "He looks good enough to eat!"

"Why don't you eat him," said Dylan. "I'd like to make my own."

Dylan had so much fun making and eating Mr. Cheesy that he didn't miss French fries at all!

"Now it's time for dessert," said Abby. She showed Dylan how to make a clock using sliced bananas and orange pieces.

Abby seemed to know a lot about healthy food, especially fruits and vegetables. Dylan never liked eating fruit before, but Abby's way of cooking made everything taste so much better.

By the end of the week, Dylan and Abby had mealtimes worked out. They would set the table by themselves. Then they would make a surprise meal for each other with Mommy's help.

Between meals, Dylan even got into the habit of munching on a carrot stick now and then.

On the last day of Abby's visit, Dylan's mommy helped him to make a special, secret dessert. She showed Dylan how to mash strawberries with a fork and put them in a plastic bowl with yogurt. Dylan stirred the mixture until it was smooth, and then his mommy put it in the freezer.

"Yum!" said Dylan when he ate the special dessert. "This is even better than ice cream!"

"And it's good for you, too," said his mommy.

When Abby's parents came back from their trip, Dylan's mommy asked them to stay for lunch.

"Please wait in the living room," she told them. "My two assistant chefs and I need room to prepare the meal!"

When lunch was ready, they sat down to a feast. And the first one to finish all the healthy food was Dylan!

"You've sure changed your mind about food in the last week, Dylan," said Uncle Robert.

"Yes, I have," said Dylan. "I love all foods now, especially fruit and funny-looking vegetables . . . even broccoli!"

Uncle Robert gave Dylan a high five. "We're all proud of you, Dylan," he said. Mommy and Abby nodded in agreement.

TEN HELPFUL HINTS

FOR PARENTS TO HELP THEIR CHILDREN EAT HEALTHY FOODS

By Dr. Richard Woolfson, PhD

1. Have realistic expectations. When you introduce your child to a new taste, give her a very small amount at a time.

2. Try not to give your child too many snacks between meals. When he returns home from school, have a few healthy, child-friendly snacks ready for him so that he doesn't eat junk food. But also make sure he eats proper meals and doesn't fill up on snacks.

3. Switch to low-fat foods when you can. Potato chips, yogurts, and cheese are all available in this format. Try to avoid deep-fried foods and use less oil when cooking.

4. Speak to your family doctor and learn about the different types of foods that your child should consume over a week.

5. Avoid dieting, for both you and your child. It's better to encourage good eating habits as a lifestyle choice than to encourage her to diet.

6. Provide your child with a choice of healthy foods to eat. He will be more interested in eating what is in front of him when he has been given some choice.

7. Try not to put too much pressure on yourself and your child during mealtimes. She will be more likely to eat if you chat and have fun than when the situation is tense.

8. Avoid making threats about eating. You should not try to force your child to eat.

9. Involve your child in preparing a meal. He could help gather ingredients, stir a mixture, or set the table. The more involvement he has in preparing the meal, the more likely he is to eat it.

10. Vary the format and presentation of foods. For example, a child who doesn't eat vegetables at dinner time might eat them when they are served as fun, finger-food snacks.

Dr. Richard Woolfson is a child psychologist, working with children and their families. He is also an author and has written several books on child development and family life, in addition to numerous articles for magazines and newspapers. Dr. Woolfson runs training workshops for parents and child care professionals and appears regularly on radio and television. He is a Fellow of the British Psychological Society.

Helping Hand Books

Look for these other helpful books to share with your child:

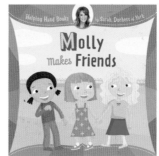